This Little Tiger book belongs to:

_____

_____

_____

_____

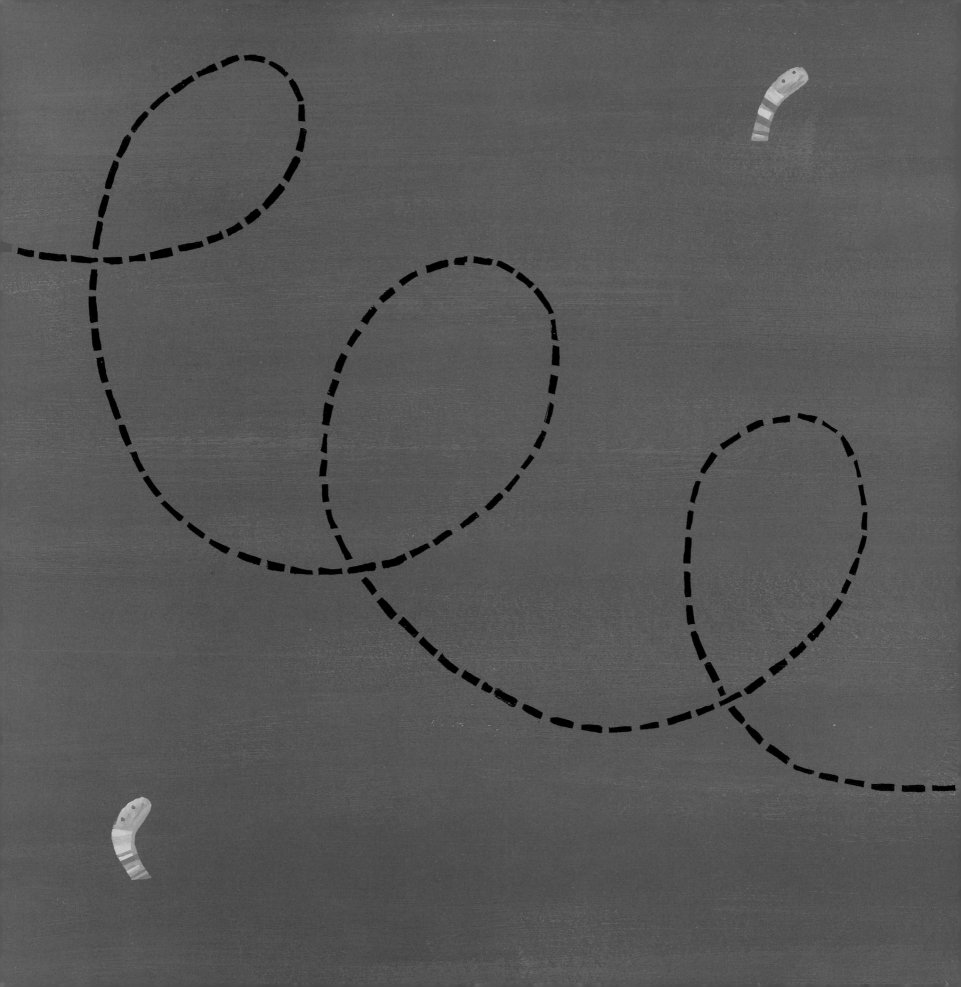

for
Toby

LITTLE TIGER PRESS

An imprint of Magi Publications

1 The Coda Centre, 189 Munster Road, London SW6 6AW

www.littletigerpress.com

First published in Great Britain 2005

This edition published 2006

Text and illustrations copyright © Jo Brown 2005

Jo Brown has asserted her right to be identified as the author and

illustrator of this work under the Copyright,

Designs and Patents Act, 1988

Printed in Spain

2 4 6 8 10 9 7 5 3 1

Hoppity Skip
Little Chick

Jo Brown

LITTLE TIGER PRESS

London

Little Chick bounced out of
bed one bright sunny morning.
"Let's play, Mum!"
he chirped.

"I need to keep these eggs safe and warm just a little while longer, Little Chick," said Mum, "but I'm sure you'll find someone to play with in the farmyard."

Little Chick tottered
outside and looked around.
Just then some geese rushed past.
"Honk honk! Follow us!"
they cried.

whiz

ZZZZZ!

Little Chick thought
that running looked fun.
So he ran too!

Little Chick tootled along –
quite fast for a little chick.

whoOooosh!

Faster and faster he ran, so fast his little chick
legs got tangled up and he tripped . . .

yeeeeEEEK!

...and skidded into a lamb! "Meeerrrr!" said the lamb. "That looks like fun, but why don't you try this?"

And she bounced
around.

boing!
Merrrr!
merrrr!

Little Chick thought
that bouncing looked fun.
So he bounced too!

BOING! Little Chick managed
a little bounce. Well, quite a big
bounce for a little chick.

He bounced . . .

and he bounced . . .

and he bounced.

He bounced so high that he whizzed through the air . . .

peeyungggg!

. . . right into a pony!
"Oops!" said the pony. "Nice bouncing, Little Chick,
now why don't you jump over this fence with me?"

And the pony jumped
straight over the fence.

Yeee-haa!

Little Chick thought
that jumping looked fun.
So he jumped too!

Little Chick did a little jump . . . then he did a bigger jump.

Then he did a REALLY
BIG jump, right over the
fence into the next field . . .

"Oops, sorry!" said Little Chick. "I need more practice landing, but jumping is great fun!"

Kersplatt!

"If you think that's fun, try this. It's luuuverly!" said the piglet, and he rolled around in the mud.

"What fun!"
thought Little Chick.
So he scritched and
he scratched . . .

and then he had
a little bit of a roll . . .

and then he did a wiggly
dusty chick dance until there
was dust everywhere.

aaaachooo!

"This is the best
fun of all!" he cried.

"Great rolling, Little Chick!" said the piglet.

"I'm having so much fun today!" said Little Chick.
"All this bouncy-jumpy-roly-running!
I can't wait to tell my mum.
See you later, Piggy!"

And he rushed
across the farmyard
to the hen house . . .

... where he had a HUGE surprise!
"Hello, Little Chick," said Mum.
"Here are your new brothers
and sisters."

And they played bouncy-jumpy-
roly-running little chick games,
all day long! And it was the
greatest fun EVER!

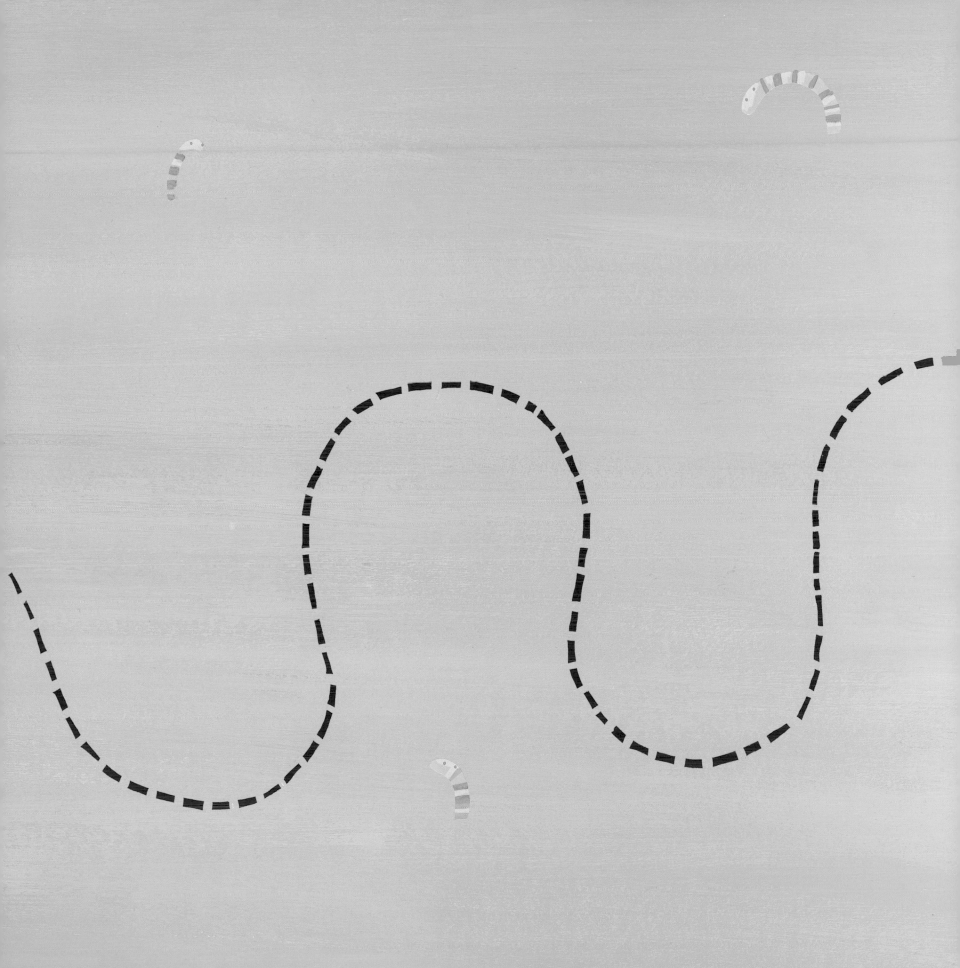

More books with bounce from Little Tiger Press

PIGS CAN'T FLY!

Ben Cort

Hopping Mad!

Michael Catchpool
David Roberts

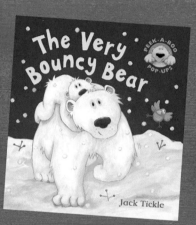

The Very Bouncy Bear

PEEK-A-BOO POP-UPS

Jack Tickle

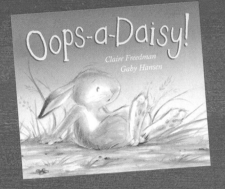

Oops-a-Daisy!

Claire Freedman
Gaby Hansen

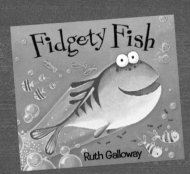

Fidgety Fish

Ruth Galloway

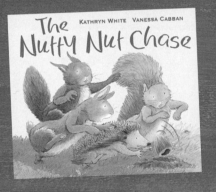

KATHRYN WHITE   VANESSA CABBAN

The Nutty Nut Chase

For information regarding any of these titles or for our catalogue,
please contact us: Little Tiger Press, 1 The Coda Centre,
189 Munster Road, London SW6 6AW, UK
Tel: 020 7385 6333 Fax: 020 7385 7333
E-mail: info@littletiger.co.uk
www.littletigerpress.com